I0683880

W
G

ISBN:1-890461-63-6

Margaret's Lucky Irish Tree

Irene Zulueta

Margaret's Lucky Irish Tree
Irene Zulueta

Published by Winlock Publishing Co.
26135 Murrieta Rd.
Sun City, Ca 92585
(951)943-0014

All rights reserved. No part of this book may be reproduced or transmitted by any form or by any means, electronic, or mechanical, including photocopying, recording or by any information storage and retrieval system without written permission from the author, except for the inclusion of a brief quotation in a review.

Copyright © 2010 by Irene Zulueta

ISBN 1-890461-63-6

Editorial assistance: Dave Galey

Associate Editor: Hal Lingerman

Luck of the Irish Tree sculpture © Lenox Corporation, 2004
For Further information about this product,
please visit www.lenox.com

Cover design: Dave Galey

Price: $11.95

CONTENTS

PROLOGUE

Many years after Santa Claus had been introduced to the world on a permanent basis, the Gilpatricks and the O'Hares maintained a residence in both Ireland and Los Angeles.

They also relived the story of Margaret and Santa Klaus through the years, as SANTA KLAUS VS. SANTA CLAUS practically became a family bible, so to speak. Not a religious bible but a book that was read each year at Christmas, just as Dicken's Christmas Carol had become a favorite in the holiday season.

The Gilpatricks and the O'Hares would bond together for the entire month, beginning at Thanksgiving and going straight through to the Christmas season; it was a gala affair.

Because Santa and Margaret had no children, there were no descendants to follow.

A growing fondness for the Gilpatricks and the O'Hares left Santa focusing his inevitable intentions on not only their families, but on future generations.

Because of this circumstance, the families decided to always name the first-born girl of a new generation, Margaret, a tradition for which the original Jayne was responsible. Be it a boy, though Santa never used his real name, the male would be called Nicholas.

Evidently, for some unknown reason his parents, who were growing older when he made his appearance, decided it was a saintly occurrence. Thus, after naming him Nicholas, they added Saint to his name, which provided him with the better known name of St. Nicholas.

However not feeling comfortable with the saint portion, they renamed him Santa. From that moment on, he was always known as Santa, even though legally, he was Nicholas Klaus.

Being the second born in the Gilpatrick family, Meagan escaped the Margaret name and as written on her baptismal certificate she became, Meagan Dorothy Gilpatrick.

Having inherited a wee bit of her great, great, great and so on, grandmother's personality, or should we say mischievousness, her first name should have been Dorothy, but with a godmother whose name was already Mary, and her cousin having been named Margaret, it seemed appropriate to start her name with an "M". Hence Meagan Dorothy Gilpatrick was what she learned to live with.

Growing older, Meagan became interested in genealogy and began tracing her family's history as far back as she was able to research. What she couldn't remember or find in her constant searches, she concocted and so goes the story of the original "Margaret and Her Lucky Irish Tree," which of course originated when Margaret was a little girl; actually happening before she met Santa Klaus.

The story everyone sat and listened to year after year in the season of Christmas was compiled in the book called, SANTA KLAUS VS. SANTA CLAUS; in her spare time, Meagan developed the story of Margaret Klaus as best she could.

Because Meagan just happened to inherit Margaret's Lucky Irish Tree, which had been carefully handed down through the years, she did not expect the facts she heard rumored. Megan wrote them to make the story not only understandable but also believable.

Who knew that one day, Meagan, would become a well known author, or would she . . .?

Read on to learn about . . .

MARGARET'S LUCKY IRISH TREE

CHAPTER ONE

Many years ago, on Margaret's ninth birthday, her parents gave her a sculpture known as "The Lucky Irish Tree."

Cherishing the tree immensely, she displayed it in a special place on the bureau in her room. Considering herself a fortunate nine year old, Margaret learned from her parents that a new ornament was to be added each year with a story to tell of its origin. This practice helped to keep her fascination with the tree alive and in suspense; Margaret never knew which or what the nature of a new decoration might be.

Being an only child, Margaret was spoiled by her parents, but one would say the spoiling was in a good way! She was polite, studious, talented, religious, well-behaved . . . Margaret had all the attributes one would dream of having in a child. These included the good attributes. Anything that appeared to be bad, her parents never mentioned.

Well, it wasn't that she was bad, it's just that she wasn't always good. Margaret was a bit on the mischievous side; but best of all was her loving nature.

The year after Margaret received her tree, she could hardly wait to see what the first ornament might be; it had been sitting barren for nearly a year.

When her parents surprised her on her tenth birthday with a leprechaun, she placed him in a very prominent position on the tree.

Naming him Terrence, Margaret told him he was the Master of the Tree.

She would have conversations with him about many things; her childhood dreams, expectations, loves, anxieties, the world away from Ireland . . . and because this was usually in the night before she fell asleep . . . , Margaret would continue their conversations into her dreams.

In one of her dreams, she actually waltzed away with Terrence onto a beautiful cloud, surrounded by a quartet of angels playing delightful music on violins.

When morning came, she quickly dismissed her seventh heaven, dressed, had breakfast and darted off to school. Being in the fifth grade at St. Adeline's, she was a straight 'A' student with only several years to go to before entering middle school.

Margaret had a lovely voice and had been playing the harpsichord for quite some time. She would write music and pretend she was an entertainer. Having an outgoing personality, she made friends quickly.

Her parents were self-employed. Margaret's father was a printer conducting business out of their home, assisted by her mother. She was often left to fend for herself; but this solitude didn't bother her. Margaret had an imagination that was out of this world and often that's where it took her. Sometimes she would even run into the woods located not too far from her home, to enjoy all the wonders of the forest, and to talk to the animals.

Margaret's Lucky Irish Tree

One night, as Margaret knelt on her knees, to say her prayers before crawling into bed, she thought she heard a voice say, "Now that's a fine lass . . . look at you . . . down on your knees praying and for what . . .? "

Stopping her prayers . . . , Margaret looked around and then continued praying. Just as she was about to finish, again, she heard the voice asking, "For what are you praying . . . I can't hear you . . . speak up . . . !"

Again, looking around, Margaret saw nothing, so she ended her prayers and crawled into bed. Coming into the room, her mother gave her a good night kiss, wished her pleasant dreams and left, closing the door behind her.

Quickly falling asleep, Margaret found herself in Dreamland where once again she heard the voice she'd heard as she was praying, asking her . . . , "For what are you praying?"

Becoming upset, Margaret looked around but she could see no one, and then the voice spoke again, only this time it called, "Margaret, I'm up here where you put me. I'm only trying to figure out what you are praying for."

At once Margaret looked toward the dresser and realized it was Terrence, the leprechaun, talking to her, inquiring about her prayers and what they meant.

When she realized he was waiting for an answer, she told him, "I'm praying for many things Terrence, don't you pray?"

Answering her, Terrence questioned, "What would I pray for Margaret? I'm only a leprechaun and I'm not even real.

I sit here on this tree where you put me, day after day, with not a worry in the world because I'm not real. Oh yes, I have a delicate sort of beauty because I'm made of fine china and someone painted me with colors to suit their taste, but that doesn't make me real. I have no soul like you; so what should I pray for?"

Answering Terrence very confidently, Margaret told him . . . "Well maybe that's what you should pray for . . . maybe you should pray for a soul . . ."

Then she said, "Oh Terrence, I'll pray for you and maybe God will hear my prayers and give you a soul with which you can truly become the master of all the other ornaments to be placed on the branches surrounding your station. Don't despair Terrence, God is everywhere, just pray and I will try to help but for now, stay with me; I'll protect you."

As Terrence came down from his place on Margaret's tree, she held him close, and as the night grew into day, Margaret heard her mother calling, "Margaret . . . Margaret, sweetheart, it's time to rise and get ready for school!"

Leaving a world of dreams behind, Margaret quickly rose, dressed, had breakfast and ran off to another day of joyous adventure at St. Adeline's School, while dismissing thoughts of . . .

THE LUCKY IRISH TREE

HAPPY BIRTHDAY, TERRY!

CHAPTER TWO

Having passed almost a year, the time for Margaret to celebrate another birthday was approaching ever so quickly.

Everyday she would get up in the morning, go to school, play at recess, make notes about homework and return home, or so it seemed. Thinking to herself, 'boring . . . boring . . ., nothing but routine,' she would go to her room for a conversation with Terrence. He was always ready to indulge himself with Maggie, a pet name he called her.

By lying down on her bed for a short nap, Margaret found this was the best way to get in touch with Terrence. Closing her eyes, it wasn't long before she saw him lift out of the nook in which he was sitting, fluff some clouds around himself and float to where she was lying.

Watching as he approached her, Margaret opened her arms to give him a wholesome hug. "And how are you today Terrence?" Margaret would ask.

Answering he told her, "Maggie, I would be a bit better if that God of yours would answer my prayers; but let's not be concerned with me . . . how about yourself. What are you up to?"

"Well Terrence, you have to have a little patience . . . ," replied Margaret. "I'm certain you are not the only one asking God for a favor.

Look at me. I've just written another song, and I've been praying for a long time, not only for you," she added so he would be aware that she was still praying for him, "but maybe, there's someone out there who would like my music . . . and just think of the good I could do if it became popular."

Knowing they both had a prayer request, without results, Terrence decided to change the subject.

"Tell me," he said, "it seems as if I've been sitting on this tree for almost a year; isn't your birthday coming up soon?"

"Why Terrence, how thoughtful of you to remember," answered Margaret. "Yes, as a matter of fact, in a couple of months I will be eleven years old," she replied. "I've told my parents I would like an animal; maybe a cat or dog. Then I would have something to keep me busy; animals don't take care of themselves."

"You do have a point," remarked Terrence; "but tell me, how would you like to have a lamb?"

"Oh Terrence, don't be so ridiculous. How could I take care of a lamb? Besides we can't keep a lamb in the house!" she replied.

Just then, there was a knock at Margaret's door, causing her to abruptly end her discussion with Terrence.

The last thing Margaret remembered hearing was her calling, Terieee, Terieee . . .," but he was gone. Lying in wait for her mother to come in to tell her it was almost dinner time, she arose without instructions.

Margaret's Lucky Irish Tree

Not hesitating to question her mother about her birthday, Margaret asked, "Mom, do you suppose I can get a lamb for my birthday?"

Being surprised at Margaret's request her mother felt shocked at such an idea but said nothing at first. Being disturbed at the thought of a lamb in the house, she suggested, "I really think a dog or a cat would be a much better choice Margaret, but I will have to discuss this idea with your father. After checking with him, we'll see what we can do!"

Several weeks passed and Margaret's birthday finally arrived. It was a very happy day for Margaret. The children in school sang and wished her a 'Happy Birthday.' Before she knew it the school day was over and the time for her celebration to begin was right after she returned home.

Entering the door Margaret saw the beautiful birthday cake setting on the table decorated with eleven candles. The wrapped presents waiting around the cake left Margaret wondering what surprises were in store for her. She could definitely tell there was no animal sitting on the table waiting to be unwrapped.

Consequently, Margaret knew the real celebrating, unwrapping presents, would begin after dinner.

Trying to be on the sly, but not the sneaky side, Margaret asked her mother if they could have an early dinner.

Of course, her mother, knowing the purpose for this consideration, couldn't help but give in to Margaret's anxiety; especially since it was her birthday. Her mother knew she would only be young once.

After finishing dinner, Margaret knew the next pleasure would be making a wish before blowing out eleven candles and devouring the cake; her choice was a piece of cake with the biggest portion of icing available. After finishing the cake she literally began attacking her presents; each gift seemed to be more in tune with her personality than the last.

Finally, coming to a small box, Margaret knew, as small as it was it could not have contained an animal. Carefully taking the ribbon from the tiny box, and not wanting to show her disappointment because there was no animal around, she allowed a smile to adorn her face as she opened the box and found a small, china lamb to hang on her Lucky Irish Tree.

Inside, she was truly disappointed, but this was her birthday and she would make the most of it. Just because she was unhappy, not to have received a pet animal, didn't mean she should make everyone else miserable.

As she asked permission to leave the table, the doorbell rang and her father excused himself to answer the door.

Retreating to her room, Margaret took the lamb directly to the tree on her bureau and found just the right place to hang it opposite Terrence.

Remembering that Terrence asked her how she would like to have a lamb, as she placed it on the tree, she said to the leprechaun, "There you are my dear! Now we both have a lamb; one to keep you company and one for me to play with in my dreams."

Margaret's Lucky Irish Tree

Interrupting Margaret's illusions, her father called her to come and see a gift that was left for her at the door!

The sound of another present sent Margaret running quickly from her room to the living room, where her parents were standing, looking at a blanket containing a hump in the middle with a shiny blue bow attached to it.

Looking at her parents, Margaret with big eyes uttered, "For me?" as she tore the cover off the object. Margaret found a bright-eyed, Miniature Schnauzer, whom she named Fancy.

Smiling her father answered, "Who else? You don't think your mother or I have the time to take care of an added member to this family?"

Margaret felt like the luckiest girl in the world.

That night when she went to sleep, bringing Terrence once more into her dreams, she told him all about her birthday surprises and she also said, "You know, Terrence, not only I had a birthday today, but you have been with me for a whole year and you too, received a birthday present, but they forgot to put your name on the box, which contained that delightful lamb meant to be your companion. So, for now I am going to say . . .

"HAPPY BIRTHDAY, TERRY!"

OMENS!

CHAPTER THREE

As the school year came to an end, Margaret and her classmates participated in a picnic. Each student received a certificate along with their report card promoting them to the next grade level. For Margaret it would be the sixth grade.

Along with the promotion to a new class, the picnic turned into a day filled with fun and games, classmate camaraderie, and the beginning of a summer filled with leisure and relaxation; not to forget about swimming in the dunking hole just outside of town. That would be the best part, but there was one other sport Margaret loved and as she grew, her parents were never reluctant to allow her to go off by herself so she could enjoy the horses that were kept at an outlying area. The owners of these horses would allow the children to ride them free of charge because they needed to be exercised.

Of course, Margaret had a favorite horse named Spooky and she along with Dennis, a classmate living down the street, would meet each day at ten o'clock in the morning and set out for the horse farm.

Having finished riding, they would go for a swim in the dunking hole and afterward would lie in the green grass, tan in the sun and exchange thoughts about their lives and futures.

Margaret didn't know for certain what she would become, perhaps an entertainer but Dennis thought he would like to be a salesman for a big company, where he would eventually rise to the heights of success and become its owner.

These were only the beginning of their dreams but dreams . . . that's where everything began, or so they thought.

Deciding it would take too many birthdays to completely fill Margaret's 'Lucky Irish Tree' her parents decided to give her the ornaments on a variety of occasions. Consequently, she had already acquired a cottage and a castle. Both ornaments were meant to give her a reason for thinking about her future.

One day, while dwelling on the motive for two ornaments recently added to her tree, namely the cottage and the castle, Margaret decided discussing them with Terry would be a good idea; after all leprechauns were suppose to be little people with big brains, or so she imagined.

That night, when Terrence let himself onto her cloud, Margaret welcomed him with her usual hug. He loved this feeling and looked forward to it each time they would visit.

While Terrence's routine was usually the same, on this occasion it was slightly different as he'd brought a companion; namely the lamb which had been acquired on Margaret's eleventh birthday. She was now twelve and almost a "teenster" as he called it.

Knowing he'd brought his lamb along, he explained before she could ask, "Smirkl needed some exercise, so I thought you wouldn't mind if he came along."

Being pleased with Terry's thoughtfulness, Margaret replied, "I'm glad you did, he's so soft and cuddly, I almost wish I'd received a lamb rather than the dog for which I asked; but don't misunderstand me. At least, I can sleep with Fancy. If I wanted to sleep with Smirkl, I'd have to sleep outside, and frankly, I prefer to sleep in my room . . ., in my bed . . . and with Fancy.

But tell me, Terry, what do you think of my two new ornaments?"

While offering Smirkl a pat on the head, he answered, "Well, if you lived in a castle you would have plenty; of room for a lamb on the inside; but if you lived in a cottage you would only be able to keep a dog. The rest is up to you and which one you would prefer."

Continuing Terrence inquired, "Margaret, would you like to see the inside of the cottage and then compare it with the castle?"

"Oh Terrence," asked Margaret, "can we do that?"

Replying Terry told her, "We'll go to the cottage, since it is farther away, but first I must return Smirkl to his branch.

Having returned the lamb to its place, they climbed toward the highest structure. Margaret realized it looked very much like the house in which she lived. After entering the front door, she found that even the inside resembled her home.

She remarked to Terry, "Why it looks just like my house .

Margaret's Lucky Irish Tree

. . It's nice to be able to see such a wonderful replica of some-thing you know actually exists; but let's get on to the castle. I'm certain it will be beautiful, but probably too expensive for me to afford," said Margaret, "unless I can sell some of my music!"

Coming down from the cottage to the castle they found, sliding down the cord while holding on to it would land them on the top floor allowing the two a way into the main portion of the building.

Finding the trap door that provided an entrance into the castle, Margaret allowed Terry to go first.

Exploring three floors of unfurnished grandeur, Margaret exclaimed, "My, how majestic! I could become accustomed to this style of living, if it were within my means."

"Oh, well, dream on," said Terrence, and as they reached the bottom floor a funnel cloud let them down as Terry settled into his nook, and Margaret woke to Fancy's chirp, knowing it was time to take her for a quick walk.

Recalling last night's adventures, Margaret wondered why of all the ornaments to be had, would she have such feelings regarding the possible domains, one a castle and one a cot-tage. Could this be an omen of what was to come . . . But why a castle?

The next time she would have an encounter with Terrence, she would have to ask him what he knew about . . .

OMENS

Irene Zulueta

A LONG TIME TO COME

Chapter Four

The summer vacation ended, and a multitude of children returned to St. Adeline's School.

The weather was beginning to cool, and the children, while concentrating on their studies, knew that in several months the season of Christmas would soon arrive.

Margaret would come home, take care of Fancy and immediately sit down to do her homework.

Her parents were totally engrossed in their business; it was at an all time high.

When Margaret ran out of daily chores to perform, she would turn to her harpsichord. She began practicing all of the Christmas hymns she knew would be sung until it was time to put them to sleep.

Wanting to discuss several ideas with Terry, Margaret found the way to her room for a short nap.

It took no time at all for Terry to fall into their regular pattern of conversation. When he asked Margaret what she would be getting for Christmas, Margaret told him she had no idea, and then asking her, "What she would like to receive," she told him, "I would like to grow up and just forget this childish stuff already. I want to be a real adult. Unfortunately, becoming a real adult is not something one can pray for . . . the rigid rules of childhood prevail, most likely with no exceptions. But tell me Terrence, do you know my friend Dennis . . . the fellow I spent my mornings with in the summer when we would go horseback riding and swimming? He's in my class at school, and the other day," she went on, "when we were in the cloak room, I don't know what possessed me, but I snuck up behind him and kissed Dennis on the cheek!"

While stopping to think about what she had done, Terry asked her, "Did you enjoy that kiss?"

Margaret replied, "Well, it was nothing special, and he didn't even kiss me back; and then Sister Mary Virginia walked in and rushed us to our desks; she was waiting to begin morning prayers. The day went on, and Dennis never said another word to me. Now I'm wondering if we are still friends."

Listening to her story, Terry told her, "Margaret, I'll tell you what you should do. If you will put me in your pocket and carry me to school with you, I will be able to see this fellow and get a better idea of what he's up to but until I can see him and observe his actions, I don't know what to tell you."

Realizing what Terry had just dictated, Margaret knew she would have to change her course of action and simply go on as if nothing had happened. Then she said to him, "Why don't we dance, rather than worry about Dennis? While waiting for a decision, Margaret watched as Terry returned to the nook from which he came and she slowly awoke to the feeling of Fancy snuggling at her side.

Trying to remember from which landscape she had descended, she awoke; her thoughts seemed to tell her, "Now is not the time for this stuff," and trying hard to remember what she discussed with Terry, she decided she should become more involved with Fancy.

Picking Fancy up as if to cradle the dog in her arms, she said, "How would you like to learn a few tricks my dear;" and off to the outdoors they went.

As she opened the door, Margaret just happened to see Dennis approaching the gate to her yard.

Immediately Margaret called out greeting him with, "Dennis, wait up." Hesitating, he listened as she continued, "I hope I didn't offend you at school today. I was only trying to let you know of the affection I feel in return for the friendship you have afforded me, and I really couldn't think of what else to do."

Having heard Margaret's explanation and, not being certain what to say . . . Dennis replied, "I sort of thought that was your implication, but when Sister Mary Virginia came into the cloak room and asked us to return to our seats, I wasn't certain what she saw or how whatever she did see could be explained, so Margaret, I really do appreciate your explanation and I do value your friendship."

Margaret now knew that she wouldn't have to worry about Terry expecting to come along with her to school. Had she waited for this moment, that discussion with Terrence, would never have taken place, but then, it made her feel good that Terry was concerned about her welfare and as far as Dennis was concerned, she hoped they would be good friends for . . .

A LONG TIME TO COME

YOUNG LOVE

CHAPTER FIVE

Resembling a soft, white blanket of velvet, the snow accompanying the season of Advent brought about a holiday spirit, thus placing everyone in a Christmasy frame of mind.

Having nothing to save but the meager allowance Margaret received from her parents by performing the chores for which they did not have time, she wondered if she had saved enough money to buy each, what might be called an 'elegant' Christmas gift. Since the big day was only a month away, she was trying to figure out how much she could realistically afford to spend for them; but what would she buy?

Being a really thoughtful person, Margaret analyzed the whole situation carefully. Perhaps she could knit a scarf for her father and maybe even one for her mother. Then possibly, she would have enough money left for two pairs of gloves to go with the scarves.

Being a very thrifty person, she took after her mother who was of Hungarian descent. Her father was an Irishman and she shared a portion of each heritage; but in her home, it was her father who ruled the roost and when her parents provided her with her next ornament, it was a replica of the Irish flag, which she placed on her tree. Her father was so proud of his Irish heritage he wanted to share it with everyone.

That night, when she went to sleep, she called on Terrence to explain the recent ornament added to her tree. Listening to her story, Terry told her, "Well, that's a neat addition, but if he feels so strongly about the flag, maybe you should give him a real one. Then he can raise it on a pole outside of the house; it might even bring in more customers. When people see it, they will say to themselves and their friends 'Now this is our countryman. We should be patronizing him with our business, he belongs here."

Listening to this explanation, Margaret interrupted Terry to question his reasoning and explained, "But what happens when they find out my mother is of Hungarian descent, which in essence . . ., sort of makes me Hungarian?"

Trying to evaluate the situation Terrence said to her, "But Margaret, look at you. You look more like your father than your mother. Who would know she is Hungarian; after all we have redheaded Irish women . . . it just happened that you got your father's genes. Consequently, you have black hair . . . and with your fair complexion you are as beautiful if not more so, than any Hungarian could be."

Blushing totally at this remark, Margaret felt a sort of satisfaction. She could hardly wait to set this conversation aside so she could look into a mirror to decide if the reflection she saw conveyed the message Terry was delivering.

Wanting to dance, Margaret told him, "Wait Terrence, I must first change my dress; these clothes are not suitable for dancing."

As she turned away to go and look for a dress, she felt a wet tongue against her cheek, and knew the culprit was Fancy, who once again slept with her through the night.

Rubbing her half-opened eyes, Margaret realized morning had come; another day was before her. Dressing quickly, she put a leash around Fancy's neck and took her walking.

Returning to her room, she glanced at her tree to make certain Terry was sitting in his usual nook. Then she remembered that in their conversation, he had suggested she buy her father a real flag.

Retrieving the money Margaret had saved from her bureau, she found just the amount needed for two pairs of gloves, yarn for two scarves, and one Irish Flag. Replacing her savings into the drawer, she returned to the kitchen where Margaret found her mother fixing breakfast.

Asking her how she and her father met, her mother told Margaret it was too long a story to tell her before school. When they had a free evening, her mother would fill her in regarding the episode of her dad and how they became acquainted.

Christmas was quickly approaching, the printing business slowed, and Margaret's mother and father closed up shop to take a much needed vacation for two weeks on into the New Year.

The day for gifts quickly came and went. Both Margaret's mother and father were pleased with the presents she had given them.

With little to do, Margaret's mother decided the day had

come when she and her husband, Frank would use this evening as an opportunity to tell Margaret the story of how the two of them had met.

Making themselves comfortable before the fireplace, Maryanna, Margaret's mother, in a loud and clear tone of voice began telling her audience . . . , which consisted only of Fancy, Margaret and her father, this mostly, unknown episode.

"It all began with a birthday party that was being arranged for your cousin, Fred's father, when he was a teenager, namely Joseph Gilpatrick. The party was going to be a gala affair.

By chance, I happened to be visiting on vacation in Ireland from Hungary and made acquaintances with the family, in the rooms next to ours, residing at the hotel. I found there was a girl named Olivia, with whom I became friends. She had been invited to a party being held for Joseph Gilpatrick's eighteenth birthday; as it turned out, there were more men attending the affair than women. Consequently, there was an urgent need to find and invite females of an adequate age group to this event. After all, the men couldn't dance with men; they definitely needed members of the opposite sex.

My friend, Olivia was asked if her friend, referring to me, would be interested in attending a gathering and I agreed to attend the affair!

Well, at first it was a daunting event, with the young men standing on one end of the room and the young girls waiting on the opposite side. Of course, having had very little training in the social graces, there wasn't one attendee who was certain of the next move. Finally, there was a fellow who was brave enough to come forward; then came another whose name was James to invite my friend Olivia to dance.

While I was feeling terribly sorry for myself, since not one of these fellows came to my rescue, and everyone was dancing with their unchosen beaus, there I stood all alone, with only one man remaining on the other end. It was inevitable that this man was meant to be my partner. What I didn't know, was that this lone man was meant to be my spouse.

We danced, never changing partners throughout the night and enjoyed one another's company to such an extent, that your father asked if he could see me again. Hardly realizing what was taking place, I agreed to see him.

After explaining to me on our first date, how he had dropped out of school to help support his family, he proceeded to tell me, work was not easy to come by. When I asked him what kind of work he did, he told me he was a printer. At the age of sixteen, I thought that was an admirable profession.

The day your father proposed to me, I was hesitant; but then I asked him, "Would there be a job whereas I could contribute my help?"

Having doubts, he asked me, "But what can you do?"

My answer to him was, "In two years I will have graduated from middle school and I could help set your type for you. It could become a family business; but first I must graduate. Then I said, "Why don't we think about it," and your father answered, "Why should we think about it, I know my desire, do you know yours?"

With that question, I told him, "Yes Frank, I know how I feel and I'd love to marry you!"

Your dad gave me a big hug and actually a great kiss on the lips to confirm what immediately became our engagement.

After graduating from middle school, I found that our love stood fast. We married and our marriage became a successful partnership in more ways than one. We earned enough money to buy a house and shortly afterward, your wee vocal chords found their way onto the scene.

Having finished the story, Margaret's mother told her, "You were such a beautiful baby! We just knew you would be an asset to our abode, and look at you Sweetheart! You have turned into everything we could have wanted and more than one can imagine and you now know our story of . . .

YOUNG LOVE"

SOMETHING BETTER

CHAPTER SIX

Spring was in the air, and time was not standing still. It seemed as if it was only yesterday that the New Year had been welcomed aboard.

As Margaret sat looking at the Shamrock adorning her tree, she reminisced and tried to interpret its meaning and why she thought clover should be planted at this time.

Being aware of the luck the clover was anticipated to provide, Margaret knew she either had to obtain some seeds, or perhaps if she went into the woods to locate some clumps of the plant, they could be dug up and brought home to transplant.

This evening when she went to bed, she would consult Terry as to where she might find transplantable clover. Certainly, he would know of a source where it could be found.

Margaret knew the reason her parents had probably given her this ornament was to enable the luck of the Irish to hopefully settle upon her in a manner befitting a believer. This was something she had learned at St. Adeline's, and it was called, faith, hope and charity. Many explanations could have been offered, but at this time all Margaret could think was, if one had faith, hope and charity, what more was needed to be lucky?

Consequently, this is what she felt the Shamrock hanging

on her 'Lucky Irish Tree' represented. In her mind, Margaret already considered herself a lucky girl; she had two wonderful parents, a delightful dog as a companion, schoolmates for friends and last but not least, Terrence whom she was beginning to consider her soul mate.

As the day neared its end with dinner over and bedtime near, Margaret made certain her homework was complete. Soon she would be in touch with Terry and this would give her a great feeling of joy.

So . . ., with a good-night kiss from her parents, it took no time at all for her to saunter into Dreamsville and quickly bring Terry onto her level.

After many conversations, Margaret found she and Terry had never discussed the bright green shamrock which was hanging so prominently on her tree. Since it had been hung close to the bottom of the tree, Margaret felt it brought the luck it was to provide, even closer to where it belonged, nearer to her heart.

However, when Margaret began to discuss the shamrock with Terrence, he quickly inquired about her intentions. He loved having it hang on the tree, close to where he sat since any rays shed by the shamrock, would hopefully bounce back toward his nook and continue to bless him with, as they all called it, 'The Luck Of The Irish.'

As it turned out, Margaret had not intended to remove the shamrock from the tree. She simply wanted to discuss an area where she might find clover that could be transplanted to her outdoor garden.

Not knowing the woodsy area she was seeking, Terrence again told her, "Margaret, if you will put me in your pocket on one of your travels to the forest, I'm certain I can help you find the clover you need."

Thinking for a moment, Margaret replied, "Terrence, it never occurred to me when I asked if you knew where I might find the plant, that you have never actually been there, so . . . how can you direct me to a specific location?"

Replying, Terry said, "Oh Maggie, I just wanted to go with you. I feel so lonely and tiresome just sitting in my nook, day after day, simply wishing and hoping that I might become real!"

Being astonished at his answer, Margaret asked him, "Terry honestly, are you still praying?"

Sheepishly putting his head down and crossing his fingers behind his back, he answered, "Well . . . when I have time!"

Feeling bewildered, Margaret asked him, "What do you mean . . . when you have time?"

Embarrassingly, he replied, "You know I have Smirkle to take care of and then I also have the watch to contend with, so no one disturbs your tree . . ."

Not caring for the explanation he gave her, Margaret declared, "This meeting is over," as she awakened and knew it was time to take Fancy for a walk.

As the aroma of pancakes and bacon arose to her nose, Margaret thought about her session with Terry, and she welcomed the opportunity to ask Dennis if he knew where in the woods she might search for clover. This would give Dennis an opportunity to share his extensive knowledge of horticulture about which he talked, as well as, the option of being able to impress Margaret.

After asking Dennis where in the woods she could find clover, and he showed her, Dennis became her hero. Having found their common denominator, they continued to spend many moments together.

Planting the greenery retrieved from the woods behind her house, Margaret watched as the clover spread and grew into large patches. It grew so beautifully that Margaret decided she would pull them apart and put them into individual pots for reproduction.

Seeing how well Margaret was doing, Dennis suggested that they start a business together; and she was really enthused about this idea.

Evidently, the shamrock hanging on Margaret's tree worked its magic and cast a wonderful spell over the two as they worked side by side, sold plant after plant, graduated from St. Adeline's and moved on into middle school. The two were inseparable until one day when Dennis came down with a terrible sickness called, Bronchitis-Pharyngitis. When the worst happened, and his sickness turned into pneumonia,

Dennis, without anyone realizing how serious it had become, died.

Being devastated, Margaret mourned his death for months. She would make her way into the forest and find a pleasant tree under which she could sit for hours; allowing the rest of the world to pass her by.

Could there ever be anyone to replace Dennis, Margaret wondered. Asking herself to where had all the precious luck she thought she had found in her garden disappeared, Margaret knew that, maybe there were more important things in store for her . . . she didn't know what, possibly. . .

SOMETHING BETTER

Irene Zulueta

ALWAYS NEAR

The sky is low, the moon is blue,
The stars aren't twinkling bright.
For you I yearn, I'll never learn,
That things aren't still alright.
Won't you see me and hear me,
Give me just one more chance?
This away . . . I can say, all the things
That my heart holds dear.
Won't you give me just one more chance dear,
To tell you, "I really care."
Go back to the start dear, and know
There will be no fear!

Somewhere I know I will find you:
Someday I hope you will care . . .
Wanting and waiting to hold you near . . .,
It is your memory that I am holding dear.

I love you, I love you, . . .with all my heart sincere,
I love you, and need you, I want you always near,
This love comes true, with dreams anew,
My heart is simply beaming, without you I'm alone,
It never may be known . . .
I love you and I need you darling,
ALWAYS NEAR!

Copyright, Irene Pichlik

SHALL WE DANCE?

CHAPTER SEVEN

For Margaret, there was no tomorrow. Realizing that she was having a hard time getting over Dennis' death, her mother decided to intervene with a new ornament; at first, Margaret was not interested.

Not having had a discussion with Terry for what seemed like a zillion years, Margaret decided it was time to renew their friendship. She really wanted to tell him about the new decoration her mother had given her in memory of Dennis, better known as the Claddagh Ring.

Actually, she wanted to know if Terrence had resumed praying, so . . . she made up her mind not to be quite so judgmental and then she would tell him all about Dennis. Margaret hoped he wouldn't mind listening. No sooner had she finished deciding that a discussion with Terrence was eminent, sleep for the night descended upon her.

Thinking about Margaret, Terrence felt her summoning him. Quickly finding a fluffy cloud on which he could float to her level, it looked as though she was ready to talk; maybe they would even try a dance or two.

Not knowing how to greet Terrence, Margaret allowed him to take the lead as she gave him a hug, and he returned the admiration. Trying to be funny Terrence said, "Long time, no talk!"

Being surprised at Terrence's expression Margaret replied, "How have you been Terry?"

Replying he confirmed his feelings with, "I'm better now that we are on speaking terms!"

Responding, Margaret admonished him with, "I'm sorry Terrence, but I was so disappointed that you weren't praying . . . , you see, one should always pray . . . not just when we want something!"

Agreeing in haste, he told her, "You know Maggie, you are so right; from here on in, I will start my day by praying. And if I pray, can we continue our relationship? I sure have missed you!" Then to Margaret's surprise, Terrence asked, "By the way, how is Dennis? Have you been seeing much of him lately?"

Feeling astonished that he would ask about Dennis, Margaret had to give this question and answer some good thought. After a bit of silence, Margaret asked if Terrence had noticed the new ornament she had placed on her tree?

Responding Terrence said, "Yes, but without having you to tell me what it meant, I disregarded the item. It is a weird looking ornament."

"Let's back up a bit Terry. If you recall, the last time we talked, I asked you about clover. With one thing leading to another, I eventually asked Dennis what he knew about clover. Knowing exactly what I was referring to, we went to the forest to find what I needed. With his expertise we gathered the necessary plants and brought them to an area behind the house; after planting them, they grew beautifully. Next we began putting them into individual pots. Since the plants were growing so well, we decided to make a business of their production."

Interrupting, Terry asked, "So I suppose, you two can be considered a 'THING' now?"

"Terrence, be patient . . . you are getting ahead of the story," remarked Margaret; but Terry's heart was pounding at what seemed like one-hundred beats a minute. That is, what he thought a heart beating one-hundred beats a minute would feel or sound like if he had one. "Okay," he replied. "So what happened?"

"Well, we moved on, and both of us graduated from St. Adeline's; we were in middle school . . ."

Once again Terrence interrupted, suggesting to her, "I'll bet he found a new girlfriend . . . I knew it . . . I knew it! Well, you had better believe, I'm going to start praying so God will make me real, and you and I can be together forever!"

Feeling it was her turn to interrupt, Margaret said, "No Terry, you don't understand."

Again Terrence's heart restarted its pounding.

Continuing, she told him, "You see, my mother gave me that ornament to ease the pain!"

Terry, thinking to himself, wondered, "Now what did he

do to her . . ., I'll kill him . . ." but he kept his thoughts to himself, as she went on.

"You see . . . This is a replica of a ring given in friendship and sometimes worn as a wedding ring. My mother was trying to help release me from my doldrums by telling me to remember all the good times we had and how we would have experienced more if we had spent our lives together.

With his heart conducting his state of mind, and not quite hearing what it was Margaret had just told him, Terrence, now practically in the midst of his own depression, very sadly inquired, "So when are you two getting married?"

Thinking for a few moments, Margaret unintentionally put Terrence in an anxious state of mind. Finally, finding the words to tell Terrence of her predicament, she blurted out, "We're not Terry. Dennis grew awfully sick and died. He simply died. All I have to remember him by is this special ring my mother gave me to bring back all my blessed memories.

So you see Terrence, you should pray while you can because one never knows when we will no longer be here to pray, for whatever we want."

Out of a clear blue sky, not knowing what else to say, Terrence ashamedly said "Margaret . . .

SHALL WE DANCE?"

HELPLESS LOVE

You've got me where you want me,
I know that you don't care,
I'm not one of your kind,
I really should beware.
But as you hold my hand,
I whisper low . . .
Kiss my lips,
And let me go.

Helpless Love, please let me go,
Helpless Love, how can I know,
Can I reveal,
All that I feel,
Or must I remain
Just another name?
Helpless Love, can you explain,
My heart aloft, feels no pain.
I am a dreamer, but realistically so.
Helpless Love, Helpless Love,
Please, let me go!

Helpless Love, is this a game?
Helpless Love, who knows no fame.
Can you hear, my appeal,
Or must I state, another claim?
Helpless Love why is it so,
You cannot let me go?
I know your memory will always reign,
Helpless Love, Helpless Love,
Please let me go!

Copyright 1943 - Irene Pichlik

Irene Zulueta

TOMORROW NEVER CAME

The night you said, "Goodbye!"
The clouds began to cry.
They cried, "Hold her close once again.
You found somebody new,
Who says he loves you too!
Now I'll never be with you Sweetheart.

There's one somebody new,
Who thinks you love him too,
My prayers remain unheard,
Now what am I to do, for . . .,

The night you said, "Goodbye,
I'll see you tomorrow . . . ,"
But tomorrow never came,
You won't be back again,
For tomorrow never came,
For our tomorrow never came!

Copyright 1976 Irene Pichlik

ALONE

CHAPTER EIGHT

Now that Terrence and Margaret understood one another, it was time for her to get on with her life.

Accepting the fact that Dennis was gone, Margaret realized that no one lives forever, and evidently, only the good die young. While considering this a good topic for discussion, she also realized it to be an avoidable subject. Thinking that, when people lived into old age meant they were not good, did not settle well in Margaret's mind; even if the quote was, "Only the good die young."

One day, when her mother grew ill, Margaret found taking care of her was a full time job, and she did the best she could. As luck would have it, it didn't rain, but it poured, or so it seemed, when her father also became ill.

Praying as she had never prayed in her life, Margaret made a point of finding the time to visit the forest for a bit of peace and solitude. It was there she prayed for her father's conversion to Christianity. Perhaps that was why her mother had recently given her a replica of St. Bridget's Cross. She was trying to make Margaret aware of something that was needed before their final moments took place. Margaret's mother was devoutly religious, but her father could only think of business.

One day, while resting under her favorite tree, Margaret, all of a sudden thought she heard a rustle in the bushes.

Thinking to herself it must be my imagination, there's no one around here but the animals, and me. Remembering it was time to check on her parents, Margaret readied herself to leave. Again hearing a rustle in the bushes she listened intently as the sound came closer. Looking around while saying to herself out loud, "What is it? Am I not alone?"

To her amazement, a voice proclaimed his presence by answering, "No my dear, you are not alone . . . you are in the presence of my company, and I am called Alex. I don't mean to disturb you, but you are sitting in a path of travel and familiarity to the persons living in this particular area. We mean you no harm . . . but what, if I may ask, is your name?"

Being startled, she told him, "My name is Margaret," while asking, "and by what may I call you?"

Answering her question, he again told her his name was, "Alex."

Wanting to know from where he came, he replied, "Well you see, I come from another dimension. I am not always alone. Sometimes there are three or four of us . . . we all have different duties, and it depends on whom each duty falls and on which day."

Thinking she understood, Margaret went on to tell him about her visits to the forest for some relaxation, as well as about her ailing parents and how it was just a matter of time before their deaths; but she would be there to care for them until the end.

Margaret's Lucky Irish Tree

Accepting her explanation Alex told her, "If there's anything I can do for you my Dear, don't hesitate to call on me."

Margaret thanked him for his courteous offer and told him, "I really have to leave now . . . " and then asked, "But will I see you again?"

Knowing what was in store for her, Alex replied, "Yes, my Dear, I will be here; just in case for some reason or other, if I am not available, there will be another by the name of Alfonso, who will also come forth in my absence. Do not be frightened, we are only here for assistance. We are working our way through a program which will be nothing but beneficial for those involved.

Thanking Alex for his courteous reply, Margaret hurried home to care for her parents; she had already been away too long.

Margaret had one great desire. Being about to finish her last year of middle school and destined to graduate in a short time, Margaret prayed that her mother and father would live long enough to see her through graduation, as that day was almost at hand.

Having arrived home in no time at all, Margaret found that a note to Dr. Doodle was in order, and though he had been taking care of her parents for some time, the time had come when there was little he could do for them; very little.

As Margaret's father lay still but conscious, he asked Margaret to remove both his and her mother's wedding rings from their fingers, as they were to be family mementos for her to cherish and keep as a remembrance of the love they had for one another.

Discussing this situation with her mother, she also told Margaret of five other boxes that contained the remaining ornaments for her Lucky Irish Tree; they were stored in a closet. A sixth box was stored overhead in a crawl space above the living room, to be kept for her future endeavors. Margaret could care less about what was stored in the attic, better known as the crawl space. All she could think about was losing two loving parents at the same time. Margaret could understand losing one, but two. Was her destiny about being alone? Being alone was all she could think of!

Margaret wanted to cry, but she knew that what was happening was inevitable; it was God's will.

That night when she retired, she knew she had to have a talk with Terrence; but sleep would not come. Cuddling close to Fancy, seemed to be Margaret's last resort.

Having lain awake most of the night, Margaret finally fell asleep, but not for long. Arising to an eerie quietness, she went to her parent's room, only to find them together at peace, but gone. The one surprise Margaret hadn't counted on, after returning to her room, was to find that evidently Fancy, for some reason, had followed her parent's path and she too was no longer with her.

For quite some time, she had been prepared for this occasion and was ready to proceed with what had to be done.

Margaret's Lucky Irish Tree

Margaret now knew the real feeling of loneliness. Putting the whole matter out of her mind, she decided the time had come to put her life in order, but which priority came first?

Basically, she knew little about her parent's business affairs; but trying to carry on with their business was definitely not her choice.

Margaret decided the best thing to do would be to consult her two cousins, Mary and Fred. She wasn't certain how they could be of help, but they knew of her situation. At an earlier time they had even offered their assistance if the need arose. Looking as if this was one of those times, she would consult them but first, Margaret needed to form a plan.

Having the proceeds from her parent's business, and since her name was on their account, worries about money were absent for now. Next were the priorities!

First, she would have to make arrangements for her parent's burial. Fortunately, their wishes had been made known to Margaret and in the process of contacting the proper authorities, she managed to fulfill her obligations with ease.

While holding a memorial service, Margaret's cousin, Mary Gilpatrick inquired about her future and even invited her to stay with the Gilpatrick's, but having a mind of her own, Margaret, with much work to be done, declined the invitation, yet leaving the opportunity open as an option.

As the days went by, Margaret decided it was time to open the five boxes stored in the closet carrying the remain-

ing ornaments for her tree. At this point, she felt there was
no special reason to save them as surprises on her birthday or
any other occasion that might arise. They would be beautiful
memories left for her provided by her parents which she could
enjoy forever.

Margaret knew that yesterday was history, today is a gift
and tomorrow is a mystery. She accepted all three ideas at a
level of profound awareness.

Already knowing her parent's history, she concentrated on
today and the gifts she found in the boxes. From these boxes,
Margaret could enjoy the comfort of her parents' spirits, who
seemed to be individually at her side. The mystery provided
for tomorrow meant she was not always . . .

ALONE

NO LONGER ALONE

CHAPTER NINE

Hesitating at first to look into the boxes given to Margaret as a final gift before her parents' demise, she finally decided the time to open them was right.

With this new availability of ornaments, after taking them out of the box, Margaret carefully hung each one in a prominent position on her tree.

Now, she thought, Terrence has a full time job of protection on call; but this matter would have to wait until later when she visited with him after dark.

Wandering around the house, Margaret had a few chores to complete, and choosing how to dispose of her parents' clothing appeared to be first on the list.

Next Margaret decided, since this inheritance was all hers, she would redecorate by painting the interior of the house; hopefully this would help to give her a cheerier disposition.

Taking care of the outdoors was a huge chore, but it had to be done, so Margaret set out to tackle this project. Besides, she needed something to keep her busy and apart from the feeling of loneliness.

Lately, when Margaret would go to sleep, even Terrence did not come to her. Evidently, with no prayers said, Terrence had simply been transposed into a figure that sat on her Lucky Irish Tree, but where was that luck when one needed it, she wondered.

Once again, her imagination assimilated a picture that made her out to be an orphan . . . a grown up orphan; but even that couldn't be right because orphans had friends, even though most were in orphanages. Poor Margaret had no friends, and the only two relatives available were Mary and Fred.

Both Mary and Fred were betrothed to someone outside of Margaret's realm. She would soon lose them to another world, one Margaret hardly imagined since Dennis' death.

The day came when Margaret who was becoming increasingly depressed decided she would look for Alex. Perhaps he could help, or at least, just talking to him might alleviate the problem.

Dressing in her most comfortable frock, Margaret set out for the area in which she would most likely find Alex.

To her dismay, she found that he was unavailable; his departure was due to a journey on which he had been assigned. However, as Alex had mentioned, there would be another to take his place. This turned out to be a fellow he called Alfonso, who was filling in for him.

Meeting him for the first time, he seemed to be an intelligent, compassionate person, and explained to Margaret about Alex's emergent mission as well as, not being certain of when he would return. The one fact Alfonso did know was that it was only a matter of time before Alex found his way back.

Telling Alfonso that she appreciated the information he

was able to impart and she would return from time to time, Margaret added, "Please tell Alex I'm sorry I missed him, but I would like to talk to him, so I can convey why I've been away for so long; I also need some of the advice I think he could give me.

Alfonso, you have been a great help and please tell Alex I will check back in a few days when hopefully he will have returned."

Starting back to her home, Margaret was carefully conspiring her next move.

There was a fair about to arrive in the outskirts of town where they would have all kinds of entertainment, food, games and contests, making it an enjoyable round of events, even for one who traveled alone.

Never having traveled anywhere by herself, Margaret decided she would call upon her cousin Mary and suggest she accompany her to this fair as a guest of honor, and she accepted.

What Margaret didn't know was that, Donald, Mary's fiance', feeling it was not safe for two women to travel alone to a festival, consequently, came along; a choice that wasn't all bad because in a gentlemanly fashion, as it turned out, he would pay all of the necessary entrance fees.

Actually, being in the company of two other people helped to make Margaret feel alive. Anticipating the actuality of the fair brought Margaret out of her doldrums. Learning that

Mary and Donald had invited Fred and his fiance' Dorothy, to join them added to the reality of the coming episode.

Margaret was overjoyed to know that the suggestion of going to the festival was not just a brief, girlish hankering; they were about to enjoy a real, fun day of friendship.

Dressing in her finest sport clothes, Margaret waited for the bell to ring. When it did, she excitedly opened the door to find Mary, and together they joined the group anxiously awaiting to continue on their way to the fair.

Margaret had not expected to find Donald had hired a buggy driver. She thought they would be walking down the road as the festival was just a short distance from the edge of town. She learned that when Donald and Mary invited Fred and Dorothy, his fiance' to come along, he'd hired this driver to deliver them right to the fair. Rather than walking, they were traveling in style by horse and buggy; how delightful this experience became.

It wasn't long before they reached the gates to the entrance, and as Fred paid the driver, Donald bought tickets for everyone.

As they passed through the gateway, the odor of food wafted through their nostrils. Margaret just knew they were going to have a joyous time.

Deciding they would like to visit the racetrack, the men left the women, since they preferred to take in some of the home improvement events; a baked goods contest was taking place, and they wouldn't miss that for anything.

However, with her love for horses, Margaret really wanted to go with the men so, telling the women of her intent, they agreed to let her go and proposed she meet them at 'The Chicken Yard' for lunch.

As Margaret made her way to the race track, she passed a number of booths with vendors showing their wares. She spied a table with a sign over it that read, "GENUINE FORTUNE TELLER-DISCLOSES ALL".

Being fascinated by the wording on the sign, Margaret advanced toward the area. As she came closer, a woman stepped out from behind an opening in a curtain, which became an entrance to a tent. Standing expressionless, the woman held out her hand to Margaret and beckoned her to come forward while at the same time, asking, "You like?"

Not knowing how to answer whatever it was this person was asking, Margaret without thinking moved forward and took her hand as the woman led her into the tent. She gently told Margaret to take a seat as she sat across from her and glared into the crystal ball that adorned the table.

Sitting quietly, Margaret listened to Gina, which the woman about to announce the fortune, called herself.

The first words Margaret heard were, "Lately there has been much sorrow in your life but for as much sorrow as you have experienced, you will be given much joy. You will be offered a job and your future will depend on whether or not you accept this work. Tell no one about this offer as they may try to dissuade you from following through. Your destiny at this point will be substantiated by those who love you, so fear not and go in peace."

Looking at Gina, Margaret repeated the words, "Go in peace! You mean that is all you have to disclose?"

Answering her, Gina said, "My Dear, were I to tell you anymore, you might have a hard time coming to a conclusion. This is a decision you must make so in the end you will know you did the right thing . . . no one will be influencing you, and that is why you will live a life of happiness."

Taking some coins from her purse, Margaret paid Gina, and went on her way as it was nearly lunchtime, and she had yet to locate 'The Chicken Yard' where they had all planned to meet for lunch.

Having finally found the girls gathered at the suggested spot, knowing she should have been accompanied by the men, they asked Margaret where they were.

Not wanting to disclose how she had become sidetracked, she told the girls, "You know, I was never able to locate them . . . the crowds were huge!"

Seeing the men quickly approaching their gathering, they waved to them and totally dropped the subject of Margaret's relocation, for which she was thankful.

Having reached the area where Dorothy was standing, Fred announced to her, "Guess what Hon?"

Margaret's Lucky Irish Tree

Before she could say anything Fred blurted out, "I won . . . I won. I had two winners and I bet on both of them."

Gazing lovingly at Fred, Dorothy inquired, "You mean you won two races?"

"No," said Fred. "I bet on two different horses in one race, and it turned out to be a photo finish, whereas they both won."

"Why Fred, that's amazing," replied Dorothy, "we should attend a fair more often. How about you Donald, how did you do?" she asked.

Boasting about his magnificent luck, Donald proclaimed, "I also won Mary, but it took me two different races . . .at least I have some of my winnings left!"

It was then Fred admitted, though he won the first race, he'd spent all his winnings on the second race, which of course he lost.

By this time, Donald told Fred, "That's okay Fred, I'll splurge for lunch; this was my idea anyway."

Standing idly by throughout the conversation, Margaret was content with the fact that no one asked how she did because, fortunately, she never made it to the track. Was this good or bad?

As far as Margaret was concerned, it was neither because it was just . . . a day at the fair, and she was . . .

NO LONGER ALONE

A NEW PROJECT

CHAPTER TEN

Having disposed of her parents' clothing at the thrift shop located around the corner from her house, Margaret was at a loss for finding new projects that needed to be taken care of.

After several weeks the excitement of the fair seemed to vanish as if it had never happened. Only Margaret knew about the fortune teller having given her an indication of her destiny.

Not having discussed the subject with anyone, she felt it weighing heavily on her mind. Even Terrence, whom she knew could be trusted, no longer came to visit; his friendship had also disappeared. Not having anyone with whom to exchange ideas, Margaret decided she would check to see if Alex had returned.

Once she reached the wooded area, Margaret learned that Alex was not available, and Alfonso again, was no where to be found. Maybe, if she sat under her favorite tree and waited for a while, someone might show up.

Putting herself in a lackadaisical, dreamy state of mind, Margaret actually fell asleep. She hadn't been sleeping for long, when she was awakened by a flutter of wings. At first, she thought it was her imagination until suddenly she heard Alfonso's voice. Peering into the shrubbery behind her and seeing no one, Margaret thought for certain, she was hallucinating until her vision brought him into sight.

Margaret's Lucky Irish Tree

Speaking up, Alfonso said, "I'm sorry, my dear, if I woke you, but when we travel long distances, we have a mode of travel we rely on to get us to our destination. My mode happens to be named Peewee. Actually, he is new to the operation, and you'll have to forgive him if he is a bit noisy."

Replying, Margaret told Alfonso, "That's okay . . . I've slept too long anyway, but I'm so glad you are here. Tell me, has Alex returned yet?"

Knowing she would ask this question, Alfonso had an answer ready and waiting for Margaret. Replying, he told her, "It shouldn't be long before Alex finds his way back here as he has another duty to perform, and there are some of us waiting for transportation so we can be delivered to our ultimate destination. Alex is aware of our vigil and the necessity to be ready to leave the moment he arrives. I might suggest Margaret, if Alex knows of your whereabouts, he will try to find you; but if you could visit at least once a day, you and Alex might happen to make contact at the same time. Then you will be saving him the effort needed to help fulfill his duty."

Listening to Alfonso, Margaret began to feel an air of mystery surrounding this whole matter. Consequently, she told him, "Visiting everyday is no problem Alfonso, I have nothing better to do, so why not. I'll come back tomorrow and everyday after so I can talk with Alex. For now, I must start for home, and thank you for being so helpful; see you tomorrow," and Margaret went on her way.

Once again, having reached home, Margaret sat down to play the harpsichord which she hadn't touched for a long time. As she played, a new melody seemed to be filtering itself into her fingers. At the same time, Margaret was remembering the time when her friend, Dennis, died. It was a rainy season, and without trying, she could just hear the words in her mind. They accompanied the melody so well, they caused her to find a pencil and paper so she could write down the words that seemed to be right in tune with the melody. However, her writing was short lived when she realized the doorbell was ringing.

Wasting no time, Margaret quickly went to the door to find her cousin Mary had come to visit. She was delighted to have company and quickly put some water on the fire for a pot of tea to accompany the box of scones Mary brought with her.

As they sat down to their treat, Margaret brought up the subject of Mary's up and coming wedding day. The discussion of Mary becoming Mrs. Donald O'Hare was really not a problem, but the question in her mind was, whom shall I ask to be my maid of honor? The choices were Dorothy or Margaret. Knowing that she and Margaret were related, Mary felt it would only be right to ask Margaret to be her maid-of-honor, and this she did.

Being thrilled to have been asked, Margaret said, "I do," almost as if she were answering a wedding vow. Realizing her inappropriate reply, Margaret commented to Mary, "Being alone so much often gets confusing when the time to talk comes along. I would love to be your maid-of-honor, just tell me what I have to do."

At this time, Mary explained to her that Dorothy, Fred's

fiance', would also be in the wedding party and that the services were to be held at St. Adeline's Church. Continuing she added, "Now, the next thing we have to do is to look for dresses, or possibly find us a dressmaker."

With this detail in mind, Margaret recommended a woman who had done a lot of business with her parents when they were alive. She told Mary, "If you'd like, I'll find her name in my parent's records. I'm certain she'll be very happy to have the business; I understand she is a capable, talented seamstress.

Knowing that Margaret was always able to grasp the importance of a situation, Mary decided to leave the matter in her hands and told Margaret she would have Dorothy call on her as there were only two of them to be involved.

When Margaret asked who their male partners would be, Mary told her that part was up to Donald. She knew Fred was going to be the best man, but she wasn't certain about who Dorothy's partner would be.

Telling Margaret she would fill her in with the details as soon as she knew them, Mary bid her farewell and returned home.

Knowing she had a lot to think about, Margaret actually gave up waiting for Alex to return.

She now had enough work to keep her busy involving . . . . . .

A NEW PROJECT

THEIR SECRET PACT

CHAPTER ELEVEN

Being asked to be part of Mary's wedding party, filled
Margaret with joy. She knew there would be many new
friendships with these soon to become relatives. Margaret
had already experienced good times with four of them at the
fair, but even with the friendliness she had encountered, she
felt that she should reach out and become even friendlier
with Dorothy. Perhaps the two of them could prepare a bridal
shower for Mary. "That's exactly what I'll do," Margaret said
to herself.

Waiting for Dorothy to call on her so they could make
plans to visit the dressmaker, whom Margaret had mentioned,
it seemed as if she was taking forever to make herself available.

Margaret finally decided to contact Mary to see if there
was a problem. She had been so definite in the decision to go
ahead with Margaret as the maid of honor; she couldn't understand what would be taking Dorothy so long to contact her.

Living not far from Margaret's home, she decided a visit
to Mary's house might be in order, just in case something
crucial had happened. Finding her way to Mary's residence,
Margaret found no one at home. With the intention of seeking
out the dressmaker, Margaret stopped home to double check
the correct address at which Madam Illustra could be found.
As luck would have it, it was a good thing she did stop to
check because as she returned to her abode, she found Doro-

thy sitting on her doorstep, waiting for Margaret to come back from wherever she had been.

After greeting one another, Margaret told Dorothy, "Had I known you were going to visit, I would not have run off so quickly; but I went to Mary's house so she could give me your address, which would have enabled me to come to you. Anyway, it's nice to see you again Dorothy, and it's a good thing too, it won't be long before Mary's big day."

Before Margaret could say another word, Dorothy interrupted and asked Margaret in a childish sort of manner, "Margaret, I have a special favor to ask of you."

Promptly answering her, Margaret questioned, "What is it Dorothy?"

Still feeling a bit sheepish, she told her, "Well, you see Margaret, Fred and I are going to be married soon after Mary and Donald, and I really wanted to be Fred's partner for Mary's wedding. I'll admit I was a bit jealous when Mary told me you had agreed to be her maid of honor, and all I could see was you and Fred walking down the aisle as we were leaving the church, and here I will be with this other guy. I don't want to be with another man; I want to be with Fred."

Interrupting, Margaret exclaimed, "But Dorothy, it's not like I am marrying Fred, he's my cousin and . . ."

Looking at her with tears in her eyes, Dorothy said, "Oh Margaret if you would let me be the maid of honor, you might be entering a new phase in your life! Just think . . . it may be you getting married next . . . well, after Fred and me that is. Can't you do this one thing, just for me? I'll never ask you for another favor."

Hesitating while Dorothy dried her tears, Margaret told her, "Dorothy, I'll tell you what! I know of a plan that might work After all, it was nice of Mary to ask me when I know you and she have been such good friends, but it's no big concern for me, whether it's you or I. If it will make you happy, here's what we can do.

First, we should go to the dressmaker and have her sew our dresses. I have a particular design I would like to see made into a beautiful gown.

Then, when we have our final rehearsal, we will play it through just as it is supposed to happen. The only difference will be, at the end of the actual ceremony in the last minute, you will slip into my place, and I will go into yours. If you follow the pattern we set at the rehearsal, then we will have fulfilled the necessary procedures."

Having finished the explanation of her plan, Dorothy gave Margaret a big hug and said to her, "I hope you will find a man as wonderful as Mary and I have discovered, because Margaret, you truly deserve one."

Feeling astonished by her acclamation, Margaret responded, "Dorothy, have you ever given any thought to your destiny?"

Answering Margaret Dorothy said, "Not really! You know

Margaret, we are born, given free will, grow up, marry a man, and have children. What other destiny is there to think of?"

"I don't know Dorothy, but when I have time to think about it, I'll let you know!", replied Margaret.

Of course, Margaret still had her thoughts set on the Fortune Teller, having disclosed nothing more than enough information to allow Margaret to come to a conclusion on her own, an ending of immense concern.

Settling the problem, regarding the prevailing situation, Dorothy and Margaret set out to visit Madam Illustra, the dressmaker of whom she spoke. Explaining her idea of design to the seamstress, Margaret could tell that she would be well pleased with her work.

Taking this opportunity to make a comment, Dorothy told her, "I wish you had explained to me what you had in mind Margaret. I could have sewn both dresses for us at a lot less expense."

Replying, Margaret at the same time inquired of Dorothy, "I wasn't aware of your expertise, Dorothy. Had I known, I would have suggested you perform the chore in the beginning."

Answering Margaret, Dorothy said, "You know, I can still do it; all we have to do is cancel the order with Madam Illustra and . . . just think of how much money we can save."

Hesitating to agree, Margaret said, "Well, I'll talk to her

and . . before she could finish her sentence Dorothy said, "I'll shop for the material tomorrow. I know you will just love what I can sew, we'll talk tomorrow!"

After Dorothy left to return home, Margaret decided she had better contact the Madam immediately.

Finding her way back to the dressmaker's shop, Margaret found the Madam had already ordered the material and there was no way in which it could be cancelled. Thanking the Madam for her time, Margaret knew her next visit would have to be with Mary.

Arriving at her home, Margaret explained the problem she had encountered with Dorothy regarding their dresses.

Having had many years of friendship with her, Mary knew exactly what Margaret was dealing with and told her, "Margaret, I know precisely how to handle Dorothy; you can simply re-confirm your order with the dressmaker; and I will take care of this whole situation. I will do it right now. "

Going in separate directions, Margaret returned to Madam Illustra's shop just as she was about to leave for the day. Telling her she wanted to re-confirm her order, the Madam was very pleased and gave her a date for their first fitting!

As Mary reached Dorothy's home, she wasted no time in telling her that Margaret was unable to cancel their order for dresses.

Trying to object, Dorothy said, "But Mary, you know I can do it!"

Margaret's Lucky Irish Tree

Trying to soften the blow, Mary replied to her, "Yes Dorothy, just like you made the dresses for the Costume Ball. I'd never told you, but I was so embarrassed to wear what you had sewn, yet I let that one slide. Donald and I simply laughed at the outcome, but this is my wedding and I will not have anything keep it from going smoothly. You had better reconsider, and Margaret will give you the date on which the two of you will have your fittings. Do we understand one another?"

Having been taken by surprise at Mary's directive, Dorothy momentarily pictured the pact she'd made with Margaret and decided she had better agree with Mary, lest Margaret decides to tell her of . . .

THEIR SECRET PACT

Irene Zulueta

GOOD FRIENDS

CHAPTER TWELVE

Having made the decision to use Madam Illustra to sew their gowns, Margaret who originally thought a bridal shower for Mary would be nice, changed her mind. Instead, she thought that she and Dorothy should take Mary out to a nice, friendly dinner several days before her wedding. Approaching Dorothy with this thought in mind, Margaret started out to her home so they could visit, as well as have an amicable chat.

Intending to ask Dorothy to help arrange the dinner for Mary, she was quite surprised at the answer Dorothy gave her.

"Oh Margaret," she said, "why would you take Mary to dinner when she'll be so busy with last minute details, she won't even be able to see straight. I really don't think that's a good idea."

Not being able to believe what she had just heard, Margaret asked Dorothy, "Well, what do you propose?"

Thinking for a long moment, she came up with, "It's too late to have a bridal shower, but how about a comfortable in-home dinner for the six of us?"

Reviewing her plan, Margaret asked, "When you say six of us, to whom are you referring?"

Replying Dorothy began by naming the six persons taking part in the wedding party and as Margaret heard the names called off, "Mary, Donald, you Margaret, and George, he's going to be your partner, Fred and myself."

At the thought of having a partner, Margaret cringed when she heard Dorothy make this statement. She remembered when they made their pact, hearing her say, "You may be entering a new phase in your life. Just think . . . it may be you getting married next!" The assertion put Margaret into a frenzied state of mind. Quietly, her visualization of this position was softly telling her, "No . . . you aren't ready to get married yet . . ., you must wait for the right man."

"Margaret," Dorothy called, as she noticed her being in a somewhat trance like state of mind . . .

Immediately, making an excuse, she answered, "Oh Dorothy, I'm sorry. I was just reminiscing about the last time I fell in love with my friend, Dennis."

Questioning Margaret, Dorothy asked, "And what happened?"

Being quick to give her a concise explanation, Margaret proclaimed, "He got sick and died." Going on she added, "I'm not ready to start a new relationship, or to get married Dorothy; this may be your thing, but it is definitely not mine."

Realizing defeat in any plan she might be concocting, Dorothy gave in and simply said to Margaret, "How about if we invite the pastor from St. Adeline's to this dinner? In this manner it will be a nice arrangement for Mary and Donald, and we can do this on the night of the rehearsal.

Agreeing with Dorothy, Margaret said, "That idea sounds good, and I'll be glad to help prepare the dinner. Shall we do this at your house or mine?"

Being happy that Margaret asked, Dorothy replied, "If you would like to do this at my house, that will be alright with me; besides, it seems as if everyone lives closer to me than they do to you."

Thinking ahead, and knowing Dorothy's personality, Margaret decided to let her handle the whole affair. She even suggested Dorothy decide on what to serve because Margaret knew that if it was a decision she made, Dorothy would either change it or have a better idea. However, there was one minor detail . . . namely, the cost. How would they manage that?

When she told Dorothy, she could handle the whole affair, Margaret was wondering just how she could bring up a discussion of the expense that would be incurred.

As Dorothy hemmed and hawed, Margaret aggressively said, "I imagine you are wondering how we are going to afford this affair, and answering her Dorothy came forward with, "You know, Fred and I have so many expenses to cover, with our wedding to take place a few weeks after Mary's, I don't know how I can afford it."

Trying to devise a solution, Dorothy came up with, "Look Margaret, it really isn't fair for you to afford the expense of decorating a house along with helping to pay for the food, so if we have this affair at your house I'll pay for the decorations and together we can do the decorating. One other thing, I'll make the cake."

For one reason or another, Margaret decided it was easier to agree with her than to try to make any changes.

Having decided on the salad, entree' and dessert, Dorothy gave the list to Margaret and told her she could have the honor of shopping for the food, since she was paying for it anyway!

Margaret couldn't believe her ears and didn't like the sound of this but what was done, was done, even if it was in an underhanded manner.

Time was moving quickly and Mary's special day was finally in sight. Dorothy and Margaret previously had completed their final fittings and the two of them were off to pick up their gowns.

Realizing she had forgotten her purse and had no money with which to pay for her dress, Dorothy told Margaret, "I think I'm going to have to come back tomorrow, because I left my money at home."

Because Margaret always believed in carrying extra cash for the sake of emergencies, she told her, "That's okay Dorothy, I have extra money with me, and I'll be more than happy to pay for your dress. You can give it back to me once you retrieve your handbag."

Inquiring Dorothy said, "Do you mind Margaret, I'll get it back to you just as quickly as Fred gives it to me."

This statement alerted Margaret to understand that she evidently hadn't forgotten her purse; Dorothy just didn't have the money to pay for her gown. Being an unusually, compassionate person, Margaret told her, "That's okay, Dorothy. When you have the money you can give it back to me."

Reaching Madam Illustra's shop, the two entered the front door. Being greeted by a sales clerk, Margaret explained, they were there to try on and pay for the dresses that were ready to be picked up.

Trying on her gown, Dorothy felt amazed at the difference it made in her appearance. She said to Margaret, "You know, I feel so beautiful, almost like a princess."

When Margaret asked Dorothy if she had chosen her wedding apparel, knowing the date she set would be several weeks after Mary's, she found Dorothy was hesitant to tell her that she hadn't even started on her preparations; she had not picked out her wedding dress nor was she ready or waiting to wear it.

Sensing there was a problem, Margaret tried to help Dorothy talk about it and she asked her, if Mary, assuming Dorothy had a wedding gown, had seen it.

Answering her very bluntly, Dorothy said to Margaret, "No, Mary hasn't seen it because there isn't one to see!"

Not quite understanding what she was trying to tell her, Margaret delved a bit further with a question having several possible answers.

"Dorothy," she asked, "Is there anything wrong between you and Fred?"

Responding quickly, she told Margaret, "No, there's nothing wrong. The real problem is, I knew if I had to buy this dress, I wouldn't be able to afford a wedding dress and now . . ."

Listening to Dorothy tell her tale of woe, made Margaret feel bad about her situation. She knew she couldn't buy Dorothy's wedding gown for her, but remarked, "You know, between the two of us, if we put our heads together, as well as our fingers, we could design it, sew it, and finish a dress in no time at all.

Listening to Margaret changed Dorothy's attitude but then, realizing she had to buy the material, she knew there wasn't even time to save the money for a purchase of this size. Dorothy knew she had to tell Margaret the truth about her predicament. Wanting to be honest with her, as the words left her lips Dorothy disclosed: "The problem is, you see, I hadn't planned on Mary getting married at the early date she chose. Then, when she gave us the date, I found there wouldn't be enough time to save the money I needed. It didn't make any difference whether I was the maid-of-honor or just another person in the wedding party; it was too soon, and I just didn't have enough money for a dress. So Fred, bless his heart told me, because Mary was his cousin, I just couldn't refuse her. Consequently, here we are to pick up a gown for which I have no money; but Fred did tell me that he would give it to me. Now you see why, this is only one of the reasons I really want to walk down the aisle with Fred. Margaret, he's such a great guy, and I'm so happy he's in love with me as I am with him."

Being the understanding person she was, Margaret said nothing because she totally understood what Dorothy was telling her. She would try to help as best she could and for now, there was nothing more to say; Margaret only needed time to think. There must be a solution to this problem she thought; we'll just play it by ear.

Saying to Dorothy, "I'll tell you what . . . Let's go looking for material first, and then we'll see if we can afford it. If we can, I'll pay for it. Whenever you feel financially able, pay me back and that will be fine with me."

Having this offer from Margaret totally surprised Dorothy, and being in an understandable state of anxiety, she found herself totally content with this suggestion. Being pleased, Dorothy knew she wouldn't have to cancel the date of her own wedding to Fred, which was several weeks after Mary's. Since Dorothy had not yet picked a maid-of-honor for her own wedding, she decided to ask Margaret to fulfill this position. Her first step would be to let Fred know of this occurrence; not only to make certain he approved of this transaction, but to let him know that she and Margaret were becoming . . .

GOOD FRIENDS

OUR LUCKY DAY

CHAPTER THIRTEEN

Completing their transaction at Madam Illustra's, Dorothy and Margaret carried their dresses home and carefully put them into a storage closet.

Telling Margaret she would leave her dress in safekeeping with her until she had paid for it, Dorothy seemed determined to have it her way.

As usual, Margaret recognized that it was easier to give in to her whims than to disagree with her.

Having finished the storage process, Dorothy went on her way after telling Margaret she would be back for the gown, just as soon as Fred gave her the money he had promised to pay for it.

With Dorothy gone, Margaret meandered around the house trying to figure out what was next on her list of priorities. Maybe she would make another trip to the woods to check on Alex, and even if he wasn't there, perhaps she could enjoy a conversation with Alfonso. He was always a delightful addition to the scenery.

Finding her way quickly to the regular area, Margaret looked around but found no one. "Well," she said to herself, "maybe I'll just sit down and relax a little, he may arrive a bit later."

As Margaret sat under her favorite tree, she began to fantasize about Mary's wedding day. As the picture in her mind unfolded, it was she at the altar getting married, but it wasn't Donald beside her; it was another man at her side. While he seemed to have quite a charming manner, she didn't recognize him; but there she was, saying, "I Do," to heaven only knows who!

Just as the minister was to pronounce them husband and wife, Margaret again awoke. Hearing Alfonso call to her from the shrubbery behind . . . she realized he had finally made an appearance.

After a short greeting, "Margaret eventually got around to asking about Alex.

After explaining her own situation, Alfonso, while listening intently, appeared to be a bit mystified, and told her, "I don't understand why he is taking so much more time than planned."

Again, listening to Alfonso describe Alex's absence, Margaret decided it was time to start for home.

Knowing her time would be limited in the next few days, as she described what would be taking place in a matter of time, Alfonso understood and wished her luck as she began the short trek home.

Having arrived, Margaret found Dorothy waiting for her to return, so she could pay for her dress with the money Fred had given her. Next Dorothy asked Margaret when she would have the time to go shopping for the material they needed for her wedding gown. Happy to hear Dorothy requesting her assistance, Margaret suggested that they first sit down and design the dress. So the two of them found a table where they could work and, literally put on their thinking caps, but once again, they hardly knew where to begin.

Thinking about the project, Dorothy offered the fact that the material should definitely be white, and then looking back and knowing how she felt when she tried on her dress at Madam Illustra's, she told Margaret, "I really think our dresses are so beautiful that if we could make my dress look something like our bridesmaid's dresses, I would be content with feeling like a princess, and then I could say, "I actually married Prince Charming, and we lived happily ever after."

In Margaret's mind, hearing the words, "Happily ever after." was followed by, "Oh if that could only be true, what a wonderful world this would be." Then she thought, if everything were happy ever after, we would never know the difference between happy and unhappy. Pitting one against the other leaves us in the middle of no where, and consequently, we have no basis for approval or disapproval, simply because we might never know the difference.

With this thought, Margaret decided it wouldn't be too terribly distasteful to be . . a little unhappy!

Ignoring her thoughts totally, Margaret suggested to Dorothy that they make her dress almost similar to the bridesmaids gown with several large bows becoming the highlights to accent the front, as well as the back, and then by all means,

Dorothy could consider her walk down the aisle noteworthy of a Princess with a Prince Charming.

Having finished the design of Dorothy's dress, the two of them set a time for shopping. The date, of course, would have to coincide with Dorothy having enough money to pay for the material, even though Margaret had presumed she would lend her the money until she could pay it back.

Meanwhile, Mary's wedding day was growing closer, and the dinner Margaret and Dorothy were to give, was to take place in the week after next.

Asking her if she had already purchased the decorations, Dorothy assured Margaret that everything needed to decorate her house had been secured.

Next on Margaret's agenda was the menu. Deciding that, since she was totally in charge of shopping, paying for and cooking the food, Margaret thought she would simply change the dinner to one she felt was more appropriate for the occasion.

Once again, deciding it would be best to have the dinner in her home, when she told Dorothy of this decision, there was no objection. To all appearances, she was perfectly content to allow Margaret to prepare the whole affair. The only problem would be in transporting the decorations as well as the cake Dorothy was going to bake.

With most problems solved, Margaret would shop for the food after she and Dorothy went shopping for material. They both decided they should check out the local thrift shop, just in case they might be having a sale on dry goods.

Entering the store, they looked around and found very little in the way of material. However, as they passed a rack of clothing, Dorothy spied a white substance that seemed to be hanging on a rack, hiding behind several items.

Telling Margaret she wanted to check out the location in which she had been attracted, they moved in that direction. Upon reaching the spot, Dorothy began pushing away the clothing that was covering the article for which she was looking, the white dress.

Pulling on the skirt, it appeared to be hung up on another item, so in her haste Dorothy pulled out two hangers, and out came two dresses. As it turned out, one was a wedding gown and the other a formal.

Seeing the two dresses put a smile on Dorothy's face and Margaret simply stared in wonderment. Expecting a comment from Dorothy, she said nothing and waited patiently.

Having been awestruck, Dorothy finally emitted her thoughts which began with, "Oh Margaret, isn't it beautiful . . . whoever do you suppose would give a dress like this to a thrift shop?"

Answering her Margaret exclaimed, "I can't imagine Dorothy, do you suppose. . . and she stopped for fear she might offend her when Dorothy spoke up and said, "I wonder if it would fit me?"

Thinking to herself, she took the words right out of my mouth, Margaret asked, "Dorothy, would you mind wearing something that has been used?"

Answering Margaret, she told her, "But it doesn't look used, and let's face it, depending on its price, I could probably never afford to buy it new! Why don't we do some inquiring. Maybe they will give it a special price and if it fits, well, I'll try it on first; maybe we could put it in lay-away!"

Taking the dress to the salesclerk, Dorothy asked if she could try it on, and she was directed to a dressing room. Margaret helped Dorothy as she put it over her head to find out that with a few alterations, it would be an almost perfect fit.

Admiring the gorgeous dress, Dorothy announced to Margaret, "Never in my wildest imagination did I ever expect to find a wedding gown in a thrift shop."

"Nor I," concluded Margaret. "Shall we see just how much it costs and exactly what the story behind this dress might be?" she asked.

"I would love to," answered Dorothy. Having removed the dress, she and Margaret trudged up to the sales counter to question the clerk.

Finishing his service with another customer he turned to Dorothy, who was holding the gown possessively and asked, "Did it fit?"

From her mouth came the words, "Almost perfectly, but

may I ask, why such a beautiful gown is in a thrift shop?"

Having expected a question like this, the clerk was ready with an answer. "One day," he went on, "a gentleman came in carrying the gown and asked me if we ever have people coming to the store, looking for a wedding dress. Telling him it was unusual, that most women want new attire, not used items, he then asked, if he were to leave this gown with me for sale, what would we charge for it?

Knowing how expensive new dresses are, I gave him a figure. Immediately, he pulled a wad of bills from his pocket, gave me the amount I suggested and announced to me, "I am going to leave this gown in your charge. You see, my fiance' was to wear it, but she was tragically killed in an unexpected accident, and I want someone who cannot afford the luxury of our means to have it, free of charge, and I hope it will bring her as much happiness as it would have brought my love, and leaving the dress behind, he left the shop."

Being totally flabbergasted as the clerk said to Dorothy, "It's yours ma'am!" Carefully wrapping the gown, the clerk handed the package to Dorothy as they thanked him for his honesty and left the store.

Looking at Dorothy, whose face was a picture of happiness, Margaret commented to her, "Wait till your Prince Charming hears this! What do you suppose he will say?"

Thinking for a moment, Dorothy told Margaret, "I hope he'll say, let's get married right away, this is . . .

OUR LUCKY DAY

A NEW HORIZON

CHAPTER FOURTEEN

The week of Mary's special day had finally shown it's face. Margaret had most of the food partially prepared for the party that she and Dorothy were planning several days before the marriage. Everyone had readied themselves for the pre-practice service to take place after the dinner.

Dorothy had filled Fred in about the exchange of partners to take place at the end of the ceremony before they returned to the vestibule of the church. Of course, Fred objected to this idea, but he also knew when Dorothy made up her mind, it was easier to go along with her, than to start an argument. Besides, he really seemed to enjoy the fact that Dorothy was all his, and he knew that he didn't like the idea of what he pictured, that is sharing her with another man, especially since she was his one and only.

The time to decorate Margaret's house was upon them, and as Dorothy arrived with only one package, Margaret asked if she had brought the decorations.

"Oh yes," replied Dorothy, "right here," and she handed the item she was carrying to Margaret. Opening the package Dorothy had provided, she found one medium sized, white bell! Not being certain what to say, Margaret asked her, "Is this it . . . one wedding bell?"

Answering, Dorothy explained, "Considering that your house isn't too large, I thought this one bell would be enough.

80

Margaret's Lucky Irish Tree

After all, you don't want to make a circus out of a wedding party. If you simply hang this bell over the table, everyone will know what it signifies and that is Mary's marriage to Donald."

Without a word, Margaret didn't approve or disapprove, but suspected the reason she felt that Dorothy didn't buy more decorations was due to of a lack of money. Settling for one wedding bell hanging from the chandelier over the dinner table, Margaret let the matter go at that.

Evening found everyone assembled, dinner was served, toasts were given and the group went on to the church for their practice session. The gentleman who was originally to be Dorothy's partner seemed to be a nice sort of fellow with good intentions until after the practice was over.

Margaret had already made her feelings known to Dorothy and Mary about her thoughts on the pattern they were trying to establish for her. Nevertheless, after the session they had decided to visit a local pub for some entertainment.

As the four of them sat at a table, to all appearances, George pulled his chair closer to Margaret with thoughts of hoping to snuggle up to her. As George came nearer, Margaret moved her chair away from him. Once again, he came closer, and with enthusiasm, put his arm around her. Margaret was thinking, what's with this guy; but he could not be discouraged. When his fingers reached her neckline and he began to tickle her ear, she finally asked him, "George, what are you doing?"

With this question George answered her, "Aw c'mon Margaret, you know you like it!"

Looking at him absurdly, she answered, "Whatever are you talking about?" Not knowing how to explain his action, George withdrew his hand from her neck, and Margaret told the group, "You know, I've had an awfully long day; I really think I would like to start for home."

Being able to see what was taking place, Mary assured Margaret they would be leaving the pub shortly.

In Margaret's mind her thoughts were filled with outrage. She couldn't even begin to imagine going with someone like George. As far as she was concerned, his manners were in very bad taste. Running through her mind were the words she had already discussed with Dorothy when she told her, "Getting married may be your thing, but until I find Mr. Right, I'm just not interested," or it was something like that, she seemed to remember.

Leaving the pub, once they reached her home, the group bid her good night and Margaret practically collapsed onto her bed as she regrouped her ideas about this thing called marriage.

Once again, Margaret was off to Dreamland, and once again she found herself at the altar saying, "I do," but still not knowing who he was. When she awoke to the dawn of a new day, Mr. Right had disappeared.

Only two days remained before Mary's days of freedom,

as she knew them would end. One day, before the wedding, Dorothy just happened to stop by to visit with Margaret; she was almost apologetic to her for what had occurred at the pub several days earlier. Margaret assured Dorothy she took no offense to what had happened, but they had to understand, she wasn't ready for an interlude leading to marriage.

Reluctantly, Dorothy told Margaret she would explain her feelings to Mary. Changing the subject, Dorothy asked Margaret what she would be wearing as an attendant for her own wedding.

Margaret then told her she would sew her own dress, and the design would be similar to the wedding gown they found for Dorothy at the thrift shop; it just wouldn't take on the appearance of a wedding dress. Drawing a sketch on paper, so Dorothy could see what Margaret had in mind, she was pleased to know she could accomplish sewing her dress with little expense and they would encounter very few problems.

Mary would be out of town on her honeymoon, and though she and Donald would return before Dorothy's wedding, Margaret, realized she was going to be the only person in the wedding party, and wondered who would be the best man. Upon questioning Dorothy, she learned it was going to be a good friend of Fred's whose name was Aloysius. Margaret was relieved to know it wasn't going to be George again!

Beginning to feel as if she was lost in time and with everything taking place all around her, she began to reminisce and realized it had been some time since she had been to the forest. Perhaps, Alex was back, and she certainly didn't want to miss an opportunity to chat with him so, with a few days remaining in her spare time, she decided a trip to the forest, where she could find Alex and Alfonso would be in order, but it was getting dark and she decided it would be in her best interest to wait until tomorrow.

Midmorning found Margaret making her way toward the location in which she knew she could find Alfonso. Fortunately, he had previously made it known that he was expecting Alex very soon. Questioning him about Alex's return, Alfonso explained they had a long distance communication, advising them of his imminent return. As the carrier pigeon who brought the message did not wait long enough for Alfonso to send a return note, he was unable to tell her anything further.

Margaret never doubted Alfonso's comment and told him, "Well if you wish to contact me, I'm not too far from here, and rather than running back and forth each day, why don't you come and visit. Perhaps I could brew us some tea, and I would enjoy having your company. You can visit anytime at all, and I welcome your friendship."

With a hug from Alfonso, Margaret said, "Farewell," as he watched her go on her way.

It wasn't long after she left that Alfonso, sitting on a stone, was feeling lonely and forlorn, when all of a sudden, he heard what appeared to be a gathering of his friends. Was Alex back, he questioned.

Thinking to himself, if only Margaret had waited . . . , what will Alex think?

Margaret's Lucky Irish Tree

Meanwhile, seeing Alfonso with his head down, between his hands, Alex called to him, and as Alfonso looked up, he saw him coming through the trees and shouted, "I thought you'd left without me."

Responding to Alfonso, Alex said, "How could I ever do that, after all, you are my friend aren't you? Friends don't leave friends, but why didn't you follow along with the rest of the guys?"

Looking at Alex with tears in his eyes of both sorrow and joy, Alfonso started to explain, "Well Alex, Margaret was here, and I had just said good-bye to her. I told her you were coming back, but I wasn't certain exactly when."

At this point, Alex told Alfonso he would wait a short time if he would get Margaret to come back so he could talk to her. Giving Alfonso instructions to reach the sleigh Alex added, "If she does not return today, I will try to get back in three or four days.

Alfonso went in one direction and Alex in another. Having reached the clearing, Alex heard a voice behind him calling, "Wait, wait. . . , Alex!"

Turning around, Alex saw Alfonso and Margaret running toward him, and he immediately ran to them.

As they headed back into the forest, Margaret felt an uncertainty about what was going to take place, as well as, a one time occurrence in process.

When Alex questioned her, Margaret quickly gave the two

of them a breakdown of recent events. First, she explained to Alex and Alfonso that both of her parents had died. Quickly she was adding that her cousin was getting married the next day . . .,

When Alex interrupted, to make it clear that he was unable to wait around long enough for a wedding to take place but he could circle back if necessary, he also explained why he needed her assistance to help a friend take care of his house-hold. A decision had to be made and it was now or . . .,

Thinking to herself, what's the difference if I disappear, Dorothy wanted to be the maid-of-honor anyway.

Remembering what she had been told upon her visitation to the fortune teller, about not being influenced by other's decisions, Margaret quickly decided she would make what appeared to be a change of destiny.

Withdrawing her hesitancy, Margaret slowly announced to Alex and Alfonso, "I know I shouldn't do this, but it is my decision, and this moment could affect the rest of my life. Besides, I have no one for whom I am responsible; I'm certain Mary and Dorothy will forgive my lack of etiquette, so . . ., out loud Margaret said, "I'm sorry Mary . . ., I'm sorry Doro-thy . . . , you will have to get married without me!" To Alex she said, "Let's go before I change my mind."

They darted off to the spot where Margaret suddenly set her eyes on Santa, his crew with all of its participants, and the sleigh attached to magnificent reindeer accompanied by Alex and Alfonso.

Margaret's Lucky Irish Tree

When Santa called, "Let's GO GUYS!" Margaret realized she was about to travel on to . . .

A NEW HORIZON

To learn about Margaret's inevitable

destiny after traveling onto a new horizon,

follow-up with "A CHRISTMAS FANTASY"

Order Blank

For the complete series of books:

Margaret's Lucky Irish Tree . . . $11.95
A Christmas Fantasy. $11.95
Santa;s In-Between Years $14.95
Santa's Second Chance $14.95
Santa's Greatest Pursuit $15.95

Send $50.00, which includes shipping and handling to:

Echoed Visions
Christmas Fantasy
P.O. Box 97
Sun City, CA 92586

Name   _____

Address _____

City, ST, Zip _____

Money Orders or checks accepted
No credit cards please

For special orders select the book and add $3 for shipping

Irene Zulueta

www.ingramcontent.com/pod-product-compliance
Lightning Source LLC
Chambersburg PA
CBHW071416170626
46811CB00003B/1421